Morning Glory: The Meadowlark's Song

written and illustrated by
Cyane D. Williams

ISBN:978:1699242698
Published by :Cyane D. Williams
F. Deane G. Williams and Wayne Drumheller, Editors
Printing Platform: KDP amazon.com

Dedicated to my fellow nestlings.

One day, a little Meadowlark named Morning Glory moved into a new tree.

She had not been out in the Great World by herself before, so the wise owl, Olivia, who lived in the top of the tree, offered to show Morning Glory around the forest. Olivia said it was very easy to find food and learn your way around.

Olivia asked Morning Glory what she liked to do best. Morning Glory said that she enjoyed singing. Olivia replied, "Oh, but that won't help you get food. I'll have to show you what to do."

Morning Glory was very excited to have a new friend.

Morning Glory met Olivia that night to go out in search of food. She tried valiantly to fly silently like Olivia, and see in the dark, but Morning Glory was not nearly as good at it as Olivia.

Olivia looked at her and said "I'm sorry, I have shown you the things I know best, and you just don't seem to have the talent for this, I cannot help you anymore."

Morning Glory went back to her own branch very sadly.

Wilson the Woodpecker heard Morning Glory crying and said "Don't worry. I'll show you how to find grubs in the trees without even having to fly, and you don't have to be quiet about it either!"

Morning Glory was so relieved, she flew up to see Wilson. He told her it was easy. She dried her eyes, glad to find a new friend to help her. Wilson asked what she liked to do, Morning Glory answered she loved to sing.

Wilson started pecking on the bark and finding the grubs underneath. Morning Glory watched him, and with his encouragement, decided to try to do the same thing. She tried to peck the bark.

"OWWWWWWWWW!! That HURT!! I bruised my beak!" she howled.

Wilson looked at her in surprise, and said, "I can't believe you can't do this. It is SO easy!" And turned back to his pecking.

Morning Glory burst into tears. She felt so rejected, all she wanted to do was sing, but no one seemed to appreciate what she thought she could do best.

From below, she heard a voice calling her. It was Phillip the Peacock, calling up the tree to offer to help her find her way around the forest. Morning Glory dried her eyes and flew down to see her new friend.

Phillip took one look at Morning Glory and said "Oh, I do not mean to be unkind, but there is really no way I could teach you to be as beautiful as I am. I get grain and food given to me because I am so glorious. I don't think you could manage to be taken care of as I am. I'm very sorry, but it's just not possible."

Poor Morning Glory was devastated, she flew up to her nest and wept. "I just want to sing. Why does everyone want me to do what they do? I can't do anything nearly as well as everyone else."

As she sat crying on her branch, Morning Glory felt a friendly wing around her shoulder. She looked up into the kind face of Matthew Mockingbird. He smiled and asked "What's the matter, Morning Glory?"

She answered "SO many things. I can't fly silently, nor peck bark, nor fan my beautiful tail; as far as I can tell" she sniffed sadly "I can't do anything right. I don't have any special gifts like they do."

Matthew was by nature a thoughtful and gentle bird, and he asked what she REALLY wanted to do. Morning Glory said "I just want to sing." Matthew laughed. Morning Glory looked hurt, but her new friend said "You're kidding me! I LOVE to sing! Let's go find some supper, then we can sing together all day!"

Morning Glory was elated. She had someone who would show her a good place to get food AND would sing with her. She wouldn't have to be quiet, get a headache, be beautiful. She could just fill up on worms and berries, then SING!! This was WONDERFUL! They went off to eat, and after they were full, Morning Glory started to hum, and Matthew joined in .

They both broke into a happy song, Matthew's voice had an impressive range. Then he heard other birds in the forest singing and he began imitating them. Morning Glory was amazed at the number of songs he could sing. But then Matthew stopped and invited Morning Glory to join him. But Morning Glory was so intimidated by his abilities, she became quite shy, and said "Oh no! My talent isn't nearly as great as yours…I can't keep up with you."

Matthew looked at her kindly, but said he had to go find some friends who would sing with him. He liked being part of a group (even if he did change parts regularly).

Poor Morning Glory felt totally alone in the forest. Night had fallen and she felt hopeless because she knew she would never learn to fly silently in the dark; nor could she peck at wood without getting a headache; and she'd never be able to strut like Phillip; even singing, which she thought was her greatest gift, she felt intimidated by Matthew.

She sat sadly in her nest and wept. She was so alone and sad that she would never find her place in the world that she cried herself to sleep.

As Morning Glory was sitting sadly in her nest, she began to feel a warmth spreading over the forest. She realized it was the sun peeking over the horizon to bring a brand new day. She watched as the light began rising over the meadow. Morning Glory thought it was the most beautiful sight she'd ever seen. Her heart was so filled with joy at the beginning of the day, she lifted her head and began to sing… the most glorious sounds came from her throat. She was singing from her heart, filled with hope and wonder at the beauty of the rising sun.

Her friends Olivia, Wilson, Phillip and Matthew all flew to her tree to listen to her beautiful song. They realized singing truly was Morning Glory's gift. She had been right all along wanting to follow her heart and sing. They finally realized they should not have tried to make her like them, but to appreciate that each and every one of them had a different gift to share.

THE END

ACKNOWLEDGEMENTS

This book has been decades in the making- I dreamt it in 1996, it is finally coming to fruition. My first thanks is to my sister-in-law, Bobbie Williams, who has been encouraging me to write this for almost the entire time. She was instrumental in finding Wayne Drumheller of the Short Book Writer's Project who kept me on task and encouraged me to illustrate the book myself. And thanks to my brother, Deane, who was my final editor and knows how children think. And to my parents, who always encouraged me to follow my dreams. I hope all who read this will remember to follow their own dreams and know they have talents to share with everyone.

Cyane Williams
Charlottesville, VA
November 2019

Made in the USA
Columbia, SC
16 March 2020